# BURNING LUST

The seduction of a Subtle woman

**TOMLIN WAYNE**

Chapter 1

She entered my office in the midafternoon, adorned in a light, patterned dress that draped over her form effortlessly like a stream. Petite and youthful, she was a touch smaller than my usual preference, yet her lengthy hair and the dress's subtle reveal of skin assured me there'd be no lack of substance to my evening meal.

Her beauty was evident, although the distress etched on her face brought to mind the aftertaste of sour whiskey, and her fleeting attempt at a smile disappeared quicker than a rabbit on a frenzied night. A tiny handbag hung from one arm, while the other clutched a bundle of documents so tight, they might have been ancient relics.

I was torn between amusement and sympathy at the scene before me, but business had been scarce, and I wasn't in a position to be choosy about prospective clients. I rose and offered her a welcoming grin, the kind I typically save for law enforcement. "Greetings from Conniel Detective Agency," I said, reaching out my hand.

As she reciprocated, the documents tumbled from her grasp, scattering across the floor by my desk. She sighed and stooped to retrieve them, revealing a glimpse of her richly toned skin that was undeniably appealing. She stood up, eyes catching sight of my old typewriter.

"Oh," she noted, fixating on it. Her gaze then shifted to me. "Do you write?"

A warmth crept into my cheeks. "Yes," I confessed, and quickly added, "That is, when I'm not busy unraveling mysteries."

Her attention returned to the typewriter, which held a solitary blank page, poised for moments of sudden creativity. I half-expected her to inquire about my writing pursuits, as most do. Instead, she surprised me. Placing the papers down, she remarked:

"Writers can be such twisted individuals, can't they?"

Her words spilled out as if she'd been suppressing them, now releasing them onto my desk like someone purging an unwanted meal. If she sought to stun me with her bluntness, she'd find no satisfaction in my reaction; I found no fault in her observation.

"What I mean is," she continued, "writers craft these tales. You dive into them and before long, you're lost. Time, day, place, even your own identity fades away. All that matters is devouring the next sentence, the next page. You're desperate to discover the finale." She shook her head. "What kind of person has the power to do that?"

"A truly twisted individual," I concurred, chuckling. "And sadly, they're in short supply. Or haven't you noticed the lack of them on the bestseller charts?" I leaned in closer. "But when you stumble upon a story that enthralls you, doesn't that make you the twisted one?"

"I suppose you're right," she chuckled, her cheeks turning a rosy shade that roughened her fine features. "Still, the blame lies with the author."

"Point taken." I nodded toward the disordered stack of papers in her grasp. "So, what brings you to my doorstep, Mrs.—?" She paused for a beat, possibly pondering how I had deduced her marital status, given the sizeable diamond adorning her left hand, which was easily worth a small fortune.

"Goffrey," she finally offered, "Glenn Goffrey."

"Alright, Mrs. Gof—"

"Just Glenn, if you don't mind."

"Glenn," I echoed, signaling her to take a seat. "How may I assist you today?"

She settled into the chair, her dress clinging to her as if it were a passionate embrace. "Mr. Conniel, I'm in need of your expertise." Her gaze stayed elsewhere, which suited me just fine as my eyes were inadvertently drawn to her shifting form.

Abruptly, she handed over the documents and suggested, "Maybe it's easier if you take a look at these first."

I thumbed through the stack without immediately delving into the text. There were about fifty unnumbered pages, double-spaced, with a uniform typeface that hinted at a computer or word processor's handiwork, likely printed with a laser printer in what appeared to be Times New Roman.

I turned back to the first page, scanning halfway through before hopping to the next. I read more thoroughly this time, then skipped ahead several pages. After a brief bout of skimming, I placed the folder down to meet her anticipatory look.

"Not too shabby," I conceded, "for those who favor this genre. The imagery is striking, the prose flows well; at a glance, the writer seems to have a penchant for the darker side of things. Yet, as with most works in this category, it can become monotonous. There's a finite number of ways to express 'love' in its physical form." Her gaze remained fixed on me. "Now, why don't you share what's troubling you, Glenn?"

"Mr. Conniel—"

"Call me Tom." I waved the papers slightly. "After perusing this, I think we can skip the formalities, right?"

"Tom." The blush crept back onto her cheeks. "The issue is the content of these pages."

"And why is that?"

She inhaled deeply, and I braced for a flood of words, but she caught me off guard again. "You've probably figured out that I'm the woman described in these writings."

I nodded, noting the descriptions were not just vivid but seemingly a precise reflection of her current state of unease. "Isn't that reason enough to be concerned?"

"Not necessarily. Some might not enjoy the explicit nature, but would relish the admiration the author clearly has for you."

"That's the problem, you see? I have no idea who the author is! And this type of attention is not what I want." She raised her hand preemptively. "And no, I haven't engaged in the acts depicted in these stories."

"Has your husband seen this? Is he aware?"

"He knows. We don't keep secrets. He's as baffled as I am. In fact..." Her voice faded.

"Go on."

"It might sound absurd, but I initially suspected he was the author. I confronted him, and it led to our first major dispute since our wedding over a year ago. He was so vehement in his denial that I backed down, yet I couldn't shake the thought that he was responsible. After all, the printouts came from our printer."

"Hold on." I raised my hand to pause her narrative. "They were printed at your place?"

"Yes, from our home office printer."

"But you're certain it wasn't your husband?"

"Absolutely not."

I felt like I was navigating a maze of confusion. "How can you be so sure?"

"As I mentioned, I suspected him too. But he was so convincing, and I wanted to trust him. If he were lying, if he wrote these things about me, it would mean I don't know the man I married at all. That's a frightening thought, isn't it?"

I gave a nod of agreement, though internally I was skeptical. From my experience, people can always surprise you, particularly those you hold dear. Yet, I had the feeling that wasn't the reassurance she was seeking.

Chapter 2

One evening, curiosity got the best of me. We had both settled into bed, and once I was certain he was sound asleep, I tiptoed up to his office. It was quiet—the computer was shut down, and the desk was clear of any documents. I double-checked that the house was secure before spending the rest of the night awake in our room, immersed in a book. My husband didn't stir at all; he was out cold. But come morning, when I peeked into his study, I discovered fresh pages about me that had seemingly printed themselves.

"Do they appear in the mornings, typically?"

"That's right."

"Was the computer on at the time?"

"No, it was off. Does that matter?"

I shrugged it off. "Not necessarily." I considered the chance of someone accessing the computer remotely. "Glenn, is your computer equipped with a modem, internet, email, and all that?"

"Of course. Doesn't everyone have those?"

I let my gaze drift as I mulled over the idea that someone could be sending these documents to her husband's printer remotely. But for what reason? A twisted form of affection?

It was time to strip it back to the basics. I refocused on Glenn, who was now preoccupied with her lap. The topic at hand seemed to have an effect on her; it was hard not to notice. One of the documents had detailed her particular fondness for a certain kind of touch during intimacy. Did her husband even know this?

"Glenn, how long into your marriage did these documents start appearing?"

She seemed jolted by the question and took a moment to respond. "Maybe six months."

"Could it be an ex or someone you were involved with before, maybe looking to stir up trouble or win you back?"

She pondered briefly before shaking her head. "No, there's nobody."

"Perhaps a stranger, or someone from work or your circle who might secretly fantasize about you?"

"No, I really don't think so. It's all so exasperating!" She articulated her frustration as if each word left a sour taste.

"Glenn, if these papers upset you so much," I motioned to the stack, "why not just throw them away? Why read them at all?" Leaning forward, her presence on my desk was undeniable. "I've tried, but I can't!" Her gaze was intense. "The initial shock and revulsion I felt when I first read them has been replaced with a strange compulsion. There are entire websites filled with this kind of material, can you believe it? I was naive to think smut was just dirty pictures or films. And it's all about me, not some fantasy character. Me!"

"That piqued your interest, made you want to read more?"

She looked away, perhaps revealing too much. "Maybe. I don't know. All I can say is that despite my resolve to ignore them, each new batch pulls me back in. I'm desperate to uncover who's behind this."

She then smiled wryly at me. "I guess I'm hooked, thanks to this sick individual."

"We're back to the beginning, then."
She was insistent. "It can't be my husband."

I offered her a smile. "A famous detective once said, 'When you eliminate the impossible, whatever remains, however improbable, must be the truth.'"

I stood up after a moment of thought. "Glenn, I think you should go home and have an in-depth conversation with your husband. It seems you both might need to address some underlying issues."

She stood up as well. "I can't do that! He was so angry when I first accused him; I was afraid he'd leave me. Please, I need your help."

Against my better judgment, I considered taking her case. On the surface, it seemed straightforward—identify the culprit and let Glenn decide what to do. But experience had taught me that cases, like people, can evolve in complex and startling ways.

However, it had been a slow month, and she was willing to pay. We agreed on terms and she left, a bit lighter on funds but with a carefree smile. Moments later, my secretary Mark popped her head in.

"So, we've got a new client?"
I flashed the cash at her. "Looks like it."
She was thrilled, playfully joking about her rent situation before snatching the money and delighting in it. I couldn't help but smile at her antics.

"What's the case about?"

I pointed to the papers scattered across my desk. "Our client has an anonymous admirer that she's not too comfortable with. She wants us to find out who's writing these."

Mark leaned in to get a better look, her interest clearly piqued. "Are these love letters? I'm a sucker for a good romance." She quickly read through the pages, her reaction turning to shock. "Who wrote this? It's quite the racy content."

She turned to me with an inquisitive look. "You're not considering accepting part of our fee in... other forms, are you?"

"No, Markie, it's strictly professional. She's just a client."

"You've been reading these, huh?"
"If you're interested, you can borrow them."

The conversation continued with Mark's usual playful banter, but I was already focused on the task at hand—unraveling the mystery of Glenn's secret admirer.

Chapter 3

Nice try, Mr. Jethro of the Pen," she teased, looming over me, her fingers playfully threatening my nether regions. "Remember the golden rule of the scribe's craft?" Her hot breath washed over me.

"Show, don't just yap about it." Her tongue launched an invasion of my mouth.

The subsequent nightfall discovered me cloaked in the gloom of an upper chamber in Glenn's abode. My expectations were nebulous, but I figured that homing in on the epicenter of the conundrum was a savvy move.

She had bided her time until her spouse was lost in slumber before ushering me in, citing his obliviousness to her consultation with me and her concerns that he'd dismiss it as frivolous and financially imprudent. She assured me she had a plan to 'deal with' any potential spousal awakening that might reveal my presence. Before I could probe into her contingency strategies, I was trailing her to the upstairs sanctum, sworn to rouse her should any eventuality arise.

I ensconced myself on an available settee, letting my gaze adapt to the penumbra. Time trudged by, and the moon's spectral beams infiltrated the space. Glenn's letters, those ardently penned missives that she claimed depicted her in uncharted territories of behavior, had me pondering my own literary pursuits and the fervor I infused within them.

What metamorphosis do we undergo in the throes of composition? Is it an irresistible urge that compels us to lay bare our most concealed ruminations for strangers' perusal? My lifelong dalliance with storytelling never prompted me to question its origins—it was as instinctive and vital as drawing breath.

Yet, in this instance, the prose fixated on Glenn, weaving narratives she swore were foreign to her lived experience. Were they mere figments of imagination or something more tantalizing?

An invitation, perhaps?

My reverie shattered at the sound from the desk. The computer had stirred to life, its screen radiating a faint luminescence in anticipation of the operating system's awakening. Across the desk, bathed in the unintended limelight, was Glenn's husband. A surge of vindication coursed through me, the kind that accompanies a hunch proven correct.

He seemed oblivious to my presence, his gaze locked on the screen, fingers poised for the word processor's cue. I found myself ensnared, options limited to either waiting for discovery or banking on his engrossment in writing to cloak my exit. Neither appealed to me.

Approaching the desk, I was at a loss for words. The predicament was decidedly awkward, and any conceivable introduction felt inadequate. But before I could muster a greeting, he swiveled and met my gaze. The words withered in my throat, his indifferent stare sending a shiver down my spine, akin to an icy tread upon my final resting place.

After a tense pause, he resumed typing. I lingered, then, without a viable alternative, I retreated, closing the door with care.

I stealthily navigated to Glenn's chamber, contemplating the enigma of truly knowing another person. As I had surmised, her husband was the architect of the salacious tales. His secrecy was his prerogative—after all, intimate secrets are the currency of relationships, as common as hidden truths within the Vatican's vaults.

The 'why' was immaterial at that juncture, a domestic puzzle for Glenn to piece together. My concern was the evidence I now possessed, ready to unveil to her. It seemed a straightforward conclusion: the spouse, in the study, with the keyboard. Case seemingly wrapped.

That conviction wavered the moment I beheld her husband slumbering beside her in the bedroom.

Bewilderment took hold as I witnessed the paradox of the man I had just observed typing now ensconced in repose. I dashed back to the study, half-expecting an empty room, a figment of my imagination. Yet, there he was, industriously typing. His productivity elicited a twinge of envy; my own writing pace was glacial by comparison.

Returning to the bedroom, I was confronted again with the dormant figure. The sensation was vertiginous, a sudden awareness of a precipice's edge without a safety net. No logical explanation presented itself—twins, clones? Specters seemed far-fetched, but for a fleeting moment, the notion of a doppelganger intruded into my thoughts.

I nudged Glenn gently. Her eyes snapped open, and I wondered how much rest she had managed to claim. Silently, she followed me into the hallway, her nightshirt draping her form in a tease of modesty.

Chapter 4

What's happened? What did you uncover?" Her gaze was comically wide, likely a reaction to my own flustered face. I gawked at her, words escaping me. A swift peek at the office, then back to her room, and I blurted out, "Glenn, is your better half in there?"

She gaped at me as if I had sprouted an extra facial feature. "Yes, that's my husband. Who else would it be?"

I ushered her toward the office and flung the door open, stepping aside for an unblocked view. "Then pray tell," I gestured to the desk, "who is that gentleman?"

Her hand clamped over her mouth at the sight of the figure at the desk. She crept forward, a blend of shock and intrigue on her face. She halted at the desk, her eyes flicking between the man and the words flickering on the screen. She uttered his name; he paused, then resumed typing with a bland look. She repeated his name, more forcefully, and began to circle the desk.

I snagged her arm. "Hold up, Glenn!" I gestured for us to exit. She trailed behind me, albeit reluctantly.

Downstairs, I remarked, "A drink wouldn't go amiss right now." She pointed to a cabinet and mumbled for me to help myself. Inside the cabinet, I found a treasure trove of fine spirits. "Fancy a tipple?" I called out, and she answered with a faint yes. I selected a bottle of aged single malt and two glasses, pouring a hefty measure for myself and a modest one for her.

I rejoined her in the living room, where she was slumped on the couch, face in hands. Handing her the glass, I quipped, "Cheers, to whatever the heck that was." I downed half my drink, savoring the burn. Some sensations, like the first drag of a cigarette or the kick of quality whiskey, are indescribable to the uninitiated.

She broke the silence. "What did we just witness?"

I shrugged. "Beats me. But unless your hubby's got a doppelganger," she dismissed the thought instantly, "we've stumbled upon the impossible."

"How can that be?"

"Your guess is as good as mine. I've never seen anything like it. Writers zoning out is one thing, but this is next level."

"Yet, you believe it, right?"

"At this juncture, Glenn, the only thing I'm dead certain of is my need for another drink." I glanced at her glass. "You good?" She nodded. When I returned, she was sitting upright, glass in lap, her nightshirt straining against her form.

"Tom," she inquired as I settled opposite her, "why'd you stop me from touching him?" I shook my head. "Just a hunch. It seemed like he was in his own world, focused solely on his writing. I feared what might happen if we disturbed him."

We sat in contemplative silence. She finally spoke, her voice soft. "What now?"

"Time to wake your husband."

"No!" Her forcefulness caught me off guard. "Not yet," she added. She downed her drink and then looked at me with newfound determination. "First, I want to read what he's written."

The office was untouched. Her husband was still engrossed in his work, crafting his latest steamy tale. Settling back into my spot on the couch, I pondered their situation. The mystery of one man in two places was baffling, but I suspected the answer lay in Glenn's reaction to his stories. Writing, especially the risqué kind, is all about seduction. A writer beckons, seeking the reader's surrender. Yet, the seduction often fails, making most books easy to abandon. Not this time, though. Glenn was utterly captivated by her husband's prose; so much so that when faced with the chance to confront him, she opted to devour his latest installment. She was, as she put it, 'hooked.'

In a twist of events, our wait was brief. The laser printer came to life with a hum, quickly warming up and dispensing pages into the tray. When the noise ceased, I observed him, half-expecting him to vanish now that his task for the evening was complete, yet he remained seated, lost in thought. Meanwhile, Glenn had navigated to his side of the desk and was now standing there, perusing his work in the monitor's light.

Chapter 5

**I** watched her expressions under the fluorescent illumination, seeing her as an expressive reader, with subtle movements of her lips and tongue, her face a canvas of ever-shifting emotions. She had barely finished the first page and started on the second when she let out a soft growl, a sound so primal it sent a shiver down my spine. I was curious about what she had read that elicited such a reaction when I noticed her husband had shifted his position.

He was now turned towards her, observing her as I was, his arm disappearing behind her. The desk and Glenn's leaning figure concealed his actions, but it was clear he was affecting her. She moaned again, struggled to keep her eyes open, and continued reading.

At her initial moan, my arousal was instantaneous; now my imagination took over, visualizing his hand caressing her, exploring her with increasing intimacy. She struggled to maintain composure as her breathing became uneven and the pages trembled in her grasp. Her husband then knelt behind her, lifting her nightshirt, and her loud groan took me by surprise as the pages fell from her grasp.

The scene unfolding was intensely erotic, reminding me of late-night soft-core films that tease but never fully reveal. Bathed in the light from the screen and the moon's soft glow, Glenn's body moved with abandon, her husband's attention holding her captive.

I saw him then, his head rising, his tongue tracing the sensitive areas of her body. He spread her apart, his tongue working diligently as she tensed at the sensation, her neck muscles standing out starkly. She braced herself on the desk, her body convulsing as she reached cliMark, her legs shaky from the overwhelming pleasure.

Without hesitation, her husband entered her. Glenn's reaction was visceral, her hands now free to express her pleasure. In one fluid motion, she removed her nightshirt, revealing her form to me completely. Her figure was as I had imagined, and she indulged in the sensations as her husband's movements matched the rhythm of their passion.

Despite the dim light, I recognized this as a scene worth witnessing. I resisted the urge to join in, reminding myself of my professional role, yet the scent of the moment was overpowering. Glenn then looked at me, her smile inviting me closer.

"Come here, Tommy," she beckoned, the name resonating with a personal history.

I rose, my movements awkward as I approached, fumbling with my belt. She brushed my hands aside, taking over with a practiced ease. Her breath was hot on my skin as she gripped me, my arousal evident.

Her "Yum" was a sound of approval as she became familiar with my form, her husband still engaged with her. Then, she welcomed me completely.

The sensation was indescribable, her mouth accommodating me, her face framed so delicately around me. It was a stark contrast to the wholesome warnings of old advertisements, but the indulgence in such primal desires was too intoxicating to ignore. Glenn was empowered by the most potent of urges, a force known since the dawn of humanity.

She met my gaze as she took me in further, her throat vibrating against me, her hands firm on me. Her eyes locked on mine, she managed to take in even more, until she was as close as physically possible.

The experience was a heady mix of taboo and exhilaration, a surrender to the base instincts we all possess. At that moment, Glenn was consumed by the sheer potency of her own sexual energy.

She eased off gradually, flaunting her finesse, allowing each new stretch of shimmering skin to slowly reveal itself in the moonlight. She devoted herself to the task at hand with vigor, her mouth working magic, her tongue fluttering wildly. At this pace, I was certain it wouldn't be long before I reached my peak. Then, her husband withdrew and redirected himself towards her other entrance.

Without breaking stride, Glenn guided my hands to her chest. I understood her silent request. Each breast filled my palm, her stiff peaks teasing my fingertips. I kneaded them, tugging at her nipples as if drawing out her essence. A moan of pleasure escaped her; she was enjoying this. Her husband pushed in, challenging her to accommodate him, and she let out a muffled cry as he entered.

Glenn braced herself against me while her husband navigated his way through her. Once fully inside, he stopped to let her adjust. A quick slap on her cheek, a wiggle in response, and he was moving again, starting slow but quickly building momentum, while she resumed her enthusiastic attention on me. None of us were going to last much longer.

The sensation hit me first, that unmistakable signal, and Glenn seemed to pick up on it too. My body shook uncontrollably, my grip on her nipples tightening, my hips thrusting involuntarily as I released into her awaiting mouth. Her husband's shout signaled his climax, his release filling her. Glenn soon followed, my release spilling onto her as she let out a scream of her own.

We spent the next few moments catching our breath, the heavy scent of our exertions hanging in the air. I began to feel a bit out of place. Glenn casually flicked some of my release from her face with a finger, contemplating it before flashing a sly grin and offering it to me.

I hesitantly accepted, allowing her to slide her finger into my mouth. She wiped it clean with a few swipes, and I held it there for a moment longer than necessary, teasing her with my tongue. Letting her go, she lingered briefly before turning back to her husband.

They turned to each other, entwining in a deep kiss. I took that as my signal to exit, tucking myself away as I left the room. On my way out, I peeked into their bedroom where her husband lay still, his breath steady, a stark contrast to the earlier frenzy.

I left their house without another drink and drove home, my mind wrestling with the night's events. The image of Glenn, the sensations we shared, they haunted me. I arrived home, my guilt mounting, questioning my professional boundaries, yet after a thorough shower, I slept surprisingly sound.

Chapter 6

The next day, Glenn reappeared, transformed and poised, exuding confidence. She stood there in a chic black dress and heels, looking every bit the part of a woman in control.

She teased about the previous night's escapades, questioning whether they hadn't been enough to inspire me. I admitted I was still processing it all. She revealed that our mutual acquaintance had left at dawn, writing more before departing, and that her husband had woken shortly after.

Her casual demeanor about the entire situation left me in contemplation, still trying to make sense of it all.

He had absolutely no recollection of his actions. "Not a single memory. He dreams every night, he tells me, yet he can't recall any of them when he wakes up," she said, locking eyes with me. "But he didn't really do anything, right?"

I met her stare without backing down. "Why me, Glenn?"

She seemed confused. "What do you mean?"

"Don't play dumb," I pressed, leaning in from across my desk. "I might have been a bit out of my mind last night, but I'm clear-headed now. You had an inkling about what we'd find in that room, didn't you? Because you had encountered him before—you'd... felt his presence before, hadn't you?"

My hand hit the desk with force. "Hadn't you, Glenn?"

She flinched as if poked by a pin. "Yes, okay! I'd seen him before," she admitted, suddenly restless, her limbs moving in a nervous dance, her skin seeming to quiver. The room fell silent, and the noise from the adjacent room ceased. When she spoke again, it was barely above a whisper.

"That night I told you about, when I stayed up—I might have dozed off, I'm not sure—but I was in our bedroom when I heard a noise from the office. My husband was sound asleep, so I went to check. Peeking through the door, I saw him, just like you did."

Her gaze was distant, haunted by the memory. "I panicked at first. But then the printer started, and I was compelled to read what was coming out. I grabbed the pages and began reading, just like last night," she said, her eyes finding mine again.

"And then I felt his touch."

She uncrossed her legs slowly, revealing more than intended, and continued to describe the experience. "His hands were familiar but also foreign. The way he touched me... my husband has never done that. He knew things about me that I didn't even understand—where and how I wanted to be touched. The pleasure kept escalating until I reached a crescendo, screaming and convulsing."

As Glenn recounted the event, the room's heat seemed to spike, and I felt sweat on my palms and elsewhere. I leaned back, hoping to hide the physical affect her story had on me.

"The intensity of that climax was like nothing I'd ever felt. It lasted forever. When I came back to my senses, he was standing, and I thought we'd move on to something else, but he guided me down to my knees."

She paused, looking down, perhaps embarrassed. "I've had my experiences before marriage, including a rough relationship. Why do some men think that roughness is appropriate both in and out of bed?"

I didn't respond, sensing the question was rhetorical.

"Turns out, I had a taste for that kind of intensity. Once you discover certain things about yourself, they don't just disappear; they wait for the right moment or person to reawaken them. And that's exactly what he did. He was gentle at first, then took control, and I was lost in the sensation, climaxing multiple times until he finished perfectly, allowing me to savor the moment."

She faced me again. "You're different, Tommy," she said, and I felt a jolt at the sound of my name. "You were raised to respect women, to treat them with care."

You were playing the role of a gentleman, weren't you? That's exactly how you acted last night, even when I was giving you oral pleasure.

Then she got up and walked over to where I was sitting. She perched on the edge of the desk, lifting her skirt to reveal her aroused state, her clitoris peeking out like a silent vow. She grabbed my hand, and as I touched her, she inhaled sharply, my finger easily sliding into her.

"I'm not a lady, Tommy," she declared, as her body eagerly responded to my touch. "You don't need to handle me with care."

I rose swiftly, pushing more fingers inside her, and she let out a gasp, her eyes closing in acceptance of the forceful entry. I moved my fingers as deep as they would go, my hand pressing against her, stimulating her. I grabbed her hair, pulling her head back until we were face to face, our lips nearly touching.

"Is this what you're looking for, Glenn? Is this the reason you came here today?" I asked.

"Yes!" she exclaimed. "Please, I need this!"

I noted her plea with a hint of irony, not having pegged her for the religious type. My fingers withdrew from her with a distinct sound, and she voiced her displeasure. Without hesitation, I brought my fingers to her lips, and she eagerly cleaned them, much like she had attended to me the previous night. It was clear she didn't just crave one thing.

But I had grown tired of Glenn's antics. I needed to get some things straight. I pulled her back to her chair, letting her tidy up before sitting down. I sat on the desk, openly displaying my arousal, and she watched intently.

"Why me, Glenn?" I inquired.

She looked at me with frustration, like someone deprived of their vice. Gradually, she regained her composure. "I knew about you," she finally said. "The detective who writes. I read about you online."

"So what?" I asked dismissively.

"Because Hammett's gone and Wambaugh didn't return my calls. I thought you being a writer could be beneficial," she explained.

"How so?"

She sighed. "Believe it or not, I was telling the truth. I started getting these letters, these stories, and they were about me. They were so captivating, I had to find out who was behind them!"

"But you had an idea of who it was before you came here."

"Yes, I did. But it seemed so implausible! I was so confused the next day. I wondered if it had all been a dream. How could it be real? Can you explain it, Tom?" I shook my head, and she continued, "So I thought maybe you could help if you came to the house, and if he appeared while you were there, then it would confirm it was real."

"And what about last night?"

"What do you mean?" Then she understood. "Last night just happened. I didn't plan to seduce you, but I enjoyed it. Didn't you?"

I felt a blush creep up my face. She was regaining her confidence. I recalled how she had looked the night before, and wondered if her sexual confidence was innate. Yet, I couldn't let her off the hook so easily.

"So, why did you come here today, Glenn? Besides seeking a divine experience, that is."

Her emerging smile turned into a scowl. "Definitely not for you, Tommy." We locked eyes, challenging each other, until she finally looked away and whispered, "I came because I still need your help."

"Why, Glenn? The mystery is solved. You know who it is, and it's not just in your head because I saw it too. That's confirmation enough for anyone."

"But I don't know how to handle it!" She was visibly shaken. "I thought you, of all people, could help me understand why he can't just... why does he have to..." She couldn't hold back her tears any longer.

I offered her tissues and returned to my desk, feeling a twinge of guilt. I sat down, letting her cry. Then, the full impact of her words hit me, and I couldn't help but laugh. She looked up, surprised by my reaction.

"I apologize," I said, regaining my composure. "I didn't mean to be insensitive. It's just that I realized you didn't hire me for my detective skills. You hired me because I'm a writer. And that's a first."

"Will you assist me?" Her smile was faint, yet it carried a glimmer of hope.

"Listen, Glenn, my being a writer doesn't grant me insight into your husband's thoughts."

"You might have some clues—"

"Let's get something straight. We writers have dual natures. I've come to terms with that. We're one person in the throes of writing, and quite another when the pen is down. Truth be told, we're often less fascinating in life than the tales we spin. The origins of our alter egos, the seeds of our stories, and the urge to write them, remain life's enigmas. Now, as for why your husband pens about things most men would rather enact, well, it's a valid query, but I'm not the one to answer it."

"Tom, remember what happened last time I confronted him about those writings—"

I raised my hand, halting her mid-sentence. "Don't confront. Demonstrate."

"Pardon?"

"It's a cardinal rule in writing, Glenn. Show, don't tell."

"I'm lost."

Switching gears, I inquired, "Ever heard of Dr. Rikky and Mr. Hyde, Glenn?"


"I haven't read it, but I think I caught the film."

Chapter 7

God, I mused. Without films, literature's classics would be long forgotten. "But you're familiar with the premise, right? Dr. Rikky, a respected doctor in Victorian England, thought he could explore his darker urges without repercussion by having his alter ego, Mr. Hyde, shoulder the blame. Only at the end does Rikky realize that he and Hyde are one and the same, inseparable from their deeds and their impacts.

"So, Glenn, given the choice between Rikky and Hyde, who would you prefer?"

It took a moment, but then understanding dawned, and her expression brightened with a smile.

"Why not have both?" she proposed.

"My point exactly." I stood and offered my hand. "Mrs. Goffrey, it seems you don't need my counsel after all."

She accepted my hand, expressing her thanks. "Mr. Conniel, I'm so grateful." She paused, eyeing a damp spot on my trousers. "Are you sure I don't owe you anything?"

"Positive."

She turned to leave but hesitated. "Oh," she said, digging into her purse, "almost forgot. Here are his latest pages. Thought you might want a look." She laid them on the desk and left with a parting smile.

I picked up the pages, noting a dark stain on one corner. Bringing it to my nose, the faint scent of Glenn's arousal was unmistakable, stirring a reaction below. Just then, Mark burst in, feigning nonchalance.

"Good Lord!" she exclaimed; eyes alight. "For a second there, I couldn't tell if you two were about to make love or war." She noticed the papers. "Ah, more reading? Perfect. I sort of ran through the last batch while you were busy."

She approached, reaching for the pages. Her other hand brushed against me accidentally, flinching at the wetness. "Yuck! What did she do, get you off through your clothes?" She sniffed her hand, then gave a sly grin. "Not bad. Better fresh, though." Her tongue flicked across her palm. "Got any more?"

I let out a low growl. That was the last straw. I had reached my limit with assertive, sensually aware women for the day. I spun her around, bending her over the desk.

"Oh!" she gasped as she was pressed down. "Wait!" she protested as I ripped away her underwear. "Those were my best—!"

But her complaint was cut short as I entered her forcefully, releasing all my pent-up frustration in a rapid, intense rhythm. My climax was swift, and I was overwhelmed by the intensity of the release. I thought I heard Mark join in my cries, but I wasn't certain.

Afterward, I was vaguely aware of Mark shaking me. "Tom," her voice was muffled, "you might need to cut back a bit, or your manhood needs a diet."

"What?" I opened my eyes, realizing I had collapsed on her. "Oh. Sorry." I pushed myself up and stumbled back into my chair, while she sat up, trying to catch her breath.

"Smooth moves there, chief," she finally quipped. "Lucky for me I was already in the zone from eavesdropping on you and that sweet young thing, or you might have done some damage." She played with the frayed edges of her destroyed undergarments. "Like what happened to these poor things."

"I'll get you new ones."

"Sure, that's what they all promise. Then before you know it, they're suggesting you go without because they're just an inconvenience and then—"

"Markie, darling," I interjected, shutting my eyes, "enough." I remained there, lounging in my seat, savoring the quiet, letting my pulse slow down.

But Mark couldn't help herself. "There's just one thing that puzzles me," she remarked. I raised an eyebrow to show her I was all ears. "What did you mean when you questioned her about who she'd prefer to live with, Rikky or Hyde?"

I briefed Mark on the prior night's events, omitting a few details. Every couple has their little secrets. I concluded, "I'm working with the theory that the man in the office and the one in her bed are two sides of the same coin. How he manages to be in two places simultaneously is beyond me, but it might indicate the intensity of his feelings for her."

Mark pondered for a bit. "So you're thinking she should confront her husband with his other half one night? Kind of a 'Pleased to meet you, can you guess who I am?'"

I shrugged. "Something along those lines."

"Show, not tell," she chuckled. "That's pretty clever, chief. But isn't that a bit dangerous?"

I agreed with a nod. "Loving someone always comes with risks. It's uncertain how Dr. Rikky will react to meeting Mr. Hyde, but Glenn seems capable of handling them both." And any other guy, I thought to myself.

I observed as Mark ceased her distraction with her panties and brought her fingers to her lips, tasting each one before putting them all in her mouth. Thoughts of Glenn crossed my mind, but Mark's laughter interrupted my daydream. "What's so amusing?" I asked.

"You," she said, her eyes twinkling. "What would an old guy like you know about love?"

Her use of the word 'love' inexplicably stirred something in me. "I might just surprise you."

"Really?"

I rose from my chair, moving toward her as my arousal grew. I took hold of her hair and positioned my other hand beneath her, still damp. She inhaled sharply, her mouth opening, and I kissed her, our tongues dancing together. After a moment, I paused and looked at her, her eyes now soft and misty.

"Well?" I prompted.

She widened her stance slightly, and I felt a trace of warmth on my fingers. She smiled, touching one hand to my lips and the other to my shoulder.

"Show," she murmured, guiding me down, "don't tell."

End